Go Ask Giorgio!

by Patricia Wittmann

illustrated by Will Hillenbrand

MACMILLAN PUBLISHING COMPANY   NEW YORK

MAXWELL MACMILLAN CANADA   TORONTO

MAXWELL MACMILLAN INTERNATIONAL   NEW YORK   OXFORD   SINGAPORE   SYDNEY

For Michael,
with special thanks to Carole

—P.W.

To Ron Harley and Olivier Dunrea,
with special thanks to Annette and Ben

—W.H.

Library of Congress Cataloging-in-Publication Data. Wittmann, Patricia. Go ask Giorgio! / by Patricia Wittmann ; illustrated by Will Hillenbrand. — 1st ed.   p.   cm. Summary: Giorgio likes to work, but he takes on so many jobs that he can no longer enjoy them. ISBN 0-02-793221-4 [1. Work—Fiction. 2. Occupations—Fiction.] I. Hillenbrand, Will, ill. II. Title.   PZ7.W78446Go   1992   [E]—dc20   91-2808

Not so long ago, in a little town in Italy, lived a man named Giorgio who liked to work.

When a car honked outside his gas station, he put on his flat blue cap and filled the car with gas. He washed the windows till they sparkled.

When it was quiet, he put on his straw hat and weeded in his garden. He liked to talk to his nanny goat.

Night was Giorgio's favorite work time. He put on his cook's hat and turned on the lights of his little cafe. All the people from town came. Giorgio sang as he dished up the slippery noodles and the spicy sausage.

If a car honked, he put on his blue cap and hurried outside. If he ran out of sauce, he put on his straw hat and picked tomatoes in the moonlight.

Giorgio and his customers were very happy.

One morning as Giorgio tied up his beans, a little boy came running into the garden.

"Giorgio, oh Giorgio! The stationmaster is sick and there's no one to take tickets. The train is coming!"

"Oh, I can do that," said Giorgio.

He took off his straw hat and ran to the station.

"Have a beeeautiful journey!" he said, taking tickets and helping people on the train.

"Giorgio, where is your hat?" someone called out.

Giorgio shrugged his shoulders.

Just as the train pulled away, the engineer tossed a hat out of
the window. It was stiff and round with gold braid. It fit perfectly.
Giorgio whistled as he walked home. Yes, he liked to work.

The very next morning as Giorgio was sweeping, the little boy ran up with a fine blue hat in his hand.

"Giorgio, oh Giorgio! The postman has to take his mother to the dentist in the city."

"But I have never delivered the mail," Giorgio said.

"Don't worry," said the little boy. "Everyone said you could do the job."

So, Giorgio put on the fine blue hat and went off to deliver the mail. The little town had narrow, curving streets. It took all morning to get the right mail to the right houses.

"Thank you Giorgio," the townspeople said.

Just as Giorgio finished, someone called out, "Giorgio, don't forget—the stationmaster is still sick!"

"Oh, yes...of course," said Giorgio. He hurried to get his stationmaster's hat and collect the tickets for the train.

When Giorgio got home he
pumped gas, weeded his garden
and cooked for the townspeople
in his little cafe. He didn't get
to sit down until the stars came
out.

"Mama mia, what a day!" he
sighed.

The next morning, before the birds had even started to sing, there was a knocking on Giorgio's window.

"Giorgio, oh Giorgio!" the little boy said. "The sardines are here. The fishermen said I should get you to help bring them in."

Giorgio was so sleepy he didn't even look at the fisherman's hat the boy handed him. The boy took Giorgio's hand and led him down to the harbor. Giorgio got in one of the shadowy boats and helped pull in the huge nets of silvery fish.

When the sun rose and the fishermen were through, all Giorgio could think of was his soft bed, but the little boy was waiting for him on the dock with a hat in each hand.

"Giorgio, oh Giorgio—" he began.

Before he could say more, Giorgio took the hats and went to work. The mail sack hung heavy from his shoulder. The streets seemed steeper than ever.

"Giorgio," one lady said, shaking her head, "this letter is for my sister, not me."

"Giorgio!" another called out. "You musn't forget to deliver this to the mayor."

When the train whistle blew, Giorgio ran to the station. He took tickets, but he didn't know who was leaving or staying. He tripped over a basket and oranges rolled all over the platform.

"Giorgio, can't you be more careful?" the conductor shouted.

When Giorgio finally got home, there was a line of cars waiting for him.

"Santa Maria!" Giorgio said, hurrying to fill them with gas. He picked his tomatoes and turned on the cafe lights just as the townspeople came to eat. Giorgio rushed into the kitchen, but his cooking did not go well.

"Giorgio, my sausage is burned," someone said.

"Giorgio, I need more noodles," said another.

Worst of all, when Giorgio tried to sing, he sounded like his nanny goat. At the end of the night he collapsed into a chair under the hats that hung on his wall.

"I don't like this at all," he said.

The next morning when the little boy knocked there was no answer. There was a sign on the door: *CLOSED*.

Cars honked, but Giorgio didn't come out.

People got hungry, but Giorgio didn't turn on his cafe lights.

"What's the matter with Giorgio?" everyone asked.

The next day, Giorgio came out of his gas station carrying a big board. With a floppy brush he began to paint. First a straw hat, then a cook's hat, and finally a flat blue cap. In black letters he wrote, *GIORGIO'S 3 HAT CAFE*. The little boy watched from behind a tree, then he ran to tell the town.

Giorgio was hanging up the sign when he saw all the townspeople walking towards him.

"Oh, dear," said Giorgio. "What do they want now?"

The mayor stepped forward.

"Giorgio we want our hats back," he harumphed.

"Of course," said Giorgio, running inside.

"Wait!" said the mayor. "If you give us back the hats you must take this last hat we have for you."

Giorgio pointed at the sign, "I only want three hats!"

"Giorgio, Giorgio," the mayor said, "we are taking back three hats. The least you can do is to take one."

Giorgio shook his head. No!
"Just look inside," the little boy said, holding out a box. "Please, Giorgio!"

Everyone was looking at Giorgio. "I'll take one look," he said, "then you can all go home."

Giorgio opened the box with a frown. He looked inside and pulled out a nightcap. It was long and green with a tassel on the end.

"Oh, my," said Giorgio.

He put it on and it fit just right. "Well, maybe I could use a hat like this."

Giorgio picked up his paint brush and changed the 3 to a 4.

The townspeople whistled and cheered.

And so it goes. If you walk by Giorgio's and see him sleeping in a hammock with a green hat on, one of the townspeople will whisper in your ear, "Shhhhh, Giorgio's hard at work."